Better Late

by Larry Gelbart

A SAMUEL FRENCH ACTING EDITION

SAMUEL FRENCH

FOUNDED 1830

NEW YORK HOLLYWOOD LONDON TORONTO

SAMUELFRENCH.COM

ISBN 978-0-573-69951-1   Printed in U.S.A.   #29763

MUSIC USE NOTE

IMPORTANT BILLING AND CREDIT
REQUIREMENTS

BETTER LATE was first produced by the Northlight Theatre in Chicago, Illinois. The performance was directed by BJ Jones, with sets by Jack Magaw, costumes by Rachel Laritz, lighting by JR Lederie, original music and sound by Rob Milburn and Michael Bodeen. The Production Stage Manager was Laura D. Glenn. The cast was as follows:

LEE . . . . John Mahoney

NORA . . . . .Linda Kimbrough

BILLY. . . . . .Steven Key

JULIAN . . . . Mike Nussbaum

This play was the recipient of the Selma Melvoin Playwriting Award, given by Northlight Theatre in Chicago, IL.

NOTE: The Northlight production used an earlier version of the script. The play has been substantially rewritten for this acting edition.

CHARACTERS

LEE BAER - A middle-aged composer, with a tongue as sharp as the mind that hones it.

NORA BAER - Four years older than Lee, his dynamic wife.

BILLY COWAN - 32. Still a child of divorce.

JULIAN COWAN - 73. Not one for going gently into the night.

SETTING

Beverly Hills and Santa Monica, California

The settings are minimal. A chair here, a table there - just enough to know our people are real and not just in a play.

TIME

The present.

AUTHOR'S NOTES

The "elegy" referred to in the script is *Goodbye for Now* by Stephen Sondheim, from the soundtrack of the motion picture, *Reds*. Larry Gelbart intended this music to be used, but other music may be substituted.

Samuel French, Inc. licenses the right to perform *Goodbye for Now* in productions of *BETTER LATE* for a separate fee. The license does not include the right to use any existing recording of the song. If *Goodbye for Now* is used, the following program credit shall be given in the same size and prominence as that accorded any other composers and lyricists listed in the credits of the program:

ACT ONE

Scene One

*(Lights up on the Baers' bedroom. **LEE** is knotting his tie, taking an occasional, anxious sip of a martini.)*

*(**NORA**, still dressing, is not having an easy time of doing it.)*

NORA. Don't.

LEE. Don't?

NORA. Don't stare at me, while I'm dressing.

(a beat, then)

I saw you. You were. You always do.

LEE. Never!

NORA. Trying to remember where a few things have shifted around? Where some of them have gone a little south?

LEE. I hadn't noticed.

NORA. *(flatly)* Uh huh.

LEE. Really.

NORA. I've noticed how often you don't.

(smoothing her dress, mutters)

Damned gravity.

LEE. Come off it, Nor. You know damned well how you've held up.

NORA. "Held up?" Run out of right-handed compliments, have we?

LEE. About half an hour into your phone call from Billy, I did.

NORA. The boy's a train wreck, how could I not talk to him?

LEE. Of course.

(The phone trills. LEE beats NORA to the receiver.)

LEE. *(impatiently, recognizing the caller's voice)* Hi…Can she call you back? We've got one foot out the door.

NORA. Is that Billy?

LEE. It's Julian.

(On NORA's cross to him:)

LEE. *(unhappily)* Nora –

(As NORA takes the receiver, a sullen LEE points to his wrist watch)

NORA. *(ignoring the gesture, into the phone)* Julian? …No problem, dear. Really, what?

(listens, then)

…Honest to God? Congratulations! That's terrific news!

(aware of LEE's growing impatience, into the phone)

Let me call you from the car.

LEE. Preferably while you're making a left hand turn into oncoming traffic.

NORA. *(into phone)* Have you called Billy? He'll be as thrilled!

(She hangs up.)

(During the following, NORA will continue dressing as LEE re-ties his tie several times, unsuccessfully trying to make its ends come out even.)

LEE. I hope you're aware that in two minutes we will have blown the curtain, thank you very much.

NORA. I'm rushing my guts out, okay?

LEE. The odd phone call to one side.

NORA. How could I <u>not</u> take his?

LEE. This is a recording.

NORA. It's not as though they ever start on time. Opening nights, especially.

*(off **LEE**'s silence)*

I can't be sorrier than sorry, okay?

LEE. Staying off the phone would be a help.

NORA. No problem.

(a beat, then)

Guess what Julian said.

LEE. I'll just eavesdrop in the car, all right?

(checking his watch again)

It's the actors I feel bad for.

NORA. For <u>all</u> the actors? Or just for poor Marla?

LEE. For <u>all</u> of them.

(miming getting to a theatre seat)

Excuse me, excuse me, excuse me. Oops. Sorry, ma'am.

(stops miming)

All while they're onstage, trying to get through the middle of the second scene.

NORA. So we'll miss what the play's about. It might be a blessing.

(attacking her dress' rear zipper)

I never minded people coming in late. I just didn't like it when they left early.

LEE. Spoken like an ex-actress.

NORA. There's no such thing.

(a beat, then)

If we get the lights, we'll be there in twenty minutes.

LEE. The whole evening's less than an hour. No one can sit still anymore. Some day each theatre seat'll have its own remote, so people'll be able to change plays. Or fast forward right through the clichés.

NORA. You afraid you'll miss her entrance?

LEE. *(ignoring that)* Can we please just get there before the reviews come out?

NORA. *(her back to him, hating to ask)* Zip me.

(As he does:)

Don't you really want to know?

LEE. Know what?

NORA. Why Julian called? How he's doing?

LEE. The truth?

NORA. Try it once.

LEE. The truth, my dear, is that somewhere in this world, there's a huge, gray rat whose cheese-ridden ass I care maybe ten times more about than however it is "dear" Julian may or may not be doing at this particular time.

NORA. Nice.

LEE. All I know is he's made us potentially a half hour late. And counting. That's without parking, if we can even find a space in the structure, which, when you do, now starts at a minimum of twelve dollars.

NORA. Did you think it was going to stay 1950 forever?

LEE. In 1950, I had a much different future in mind. It was a lot cheaper, far less crowded, and -

(rechecking his watch)

- We got to wherever we were going when we agreed we were supposed to.

NORA. Didn't get much work done today, right?

LEE. I got a lot of work done. I wrote almost half the second movement before I realized Leonard Bernstein wrote it first. Beware of ideas that come to you whole and complete.

(knowing her look)

What?

NORA. Nothing.

LEE. Except?

NORA. How do you know what scene they're going to be in the middle of when we get there? Have you been running lines with someone?

LEE. *(annoyed)* I read the play.

NORA. Where'd you get it?

LEE. I read the published version.

NORA. Since when do you read plays before we go see them?

LEE. Since every actor in the world started mumbling.

NORA. *(softly)* What'd you say?

LEE. Since every actor started – very funny.

NORA. I think maybe you're <u>hearing</u> mumbles. Or <u>not</u> hearing them, as the case may be.

LEE. We took the same hearing test last week. My hearing's just fine. I could hear you flunking yours in the next office.

NORA. Yours is completely selective. You only hear what you want to hear.

LEE. Unlike everyone else?

(adds)

Oh, and about Marla? You know good and well I haven't seen from her or heard from her since we <u>both</u> ran into her at Jerry Pollack's Oscar party.

NORA. There've been no phone calls?

LEE. *(sighs)* No phone calls. No e-mails. No smoke signals, no tom-toms, no carrier pigeons! For God's sake, is it impossible for us to go twenty-four hours without getting into her?

NORA. You tell me.

LEE. Look. It's as over as I've sworn over and over it is. Every last, precious bit of me is as yours alone as it can be. You ready?

NORA. So I can understand –

LEE. One postmortem for the road?

NORA. What did she mean to you? I mean, really. What was it, the lure of the hunt? The thrill of coming to someone whole and new, flawless? The pleasure of a never-before-lied-to-clean-slate?

LEE. Whatever it was, the past is exactly the right tense.

NORA. You get a little rusty at believing, you know?

LEE. *(a beat; then, giving up on his tie)* It's such a drag going to the theatre in L.A.

NORA. Say the word, we've got meatloaf.

LEE. *(mutters)* I detest putting on a tie while the sun's still up.

NORA. No one's making you wear one.

LEE. I want to wear a tie when I go to the theatre. It's generational. I'm stuck. Did you notice at Herb's funeral how many guys didn't wear one?

NORA. Herb must have been furious.

LEE. Same thing at Arnie Ross'. Somebody dies nowadays, people get dressed for a demolition derby.

NORA. You're the one who doesn't like to put on a tie when the sun's still up.

LEE. For a play! This is death we're talking about! It's a sign of respect.

NORA. It's a sign of being uncomfortable.

LEE. Life is uncomfortable.

NORA. Nothing is fun for you anymore unless it's tortured.

LEE. Save the gratuitous therapy for the car, okay?

(a beat, then)

I want everyone wearing a tie when I go. Including me.

NORA. I'll make a note.

*(**LEE** checks his watch again.)*

NORA. *(selecting jewelry)* Two seconds.

LEE. You don't need a watch.

(a beat, then)

Ever.

NORA. *(strapping a watch on)* I just hope she's playing a Nazi.

LEE. It's a play about Thomas Edison. There weren't too many Nazis running around Menlo Park.

NORA. I swear, if we didn't have to meet the Bergmans, subscription or no ...

LEE. Meatloaf's fine with me.

NORA. *(donning a bracelet)* So? You not the least bit curious? You don't want to know how Julian is?

LEE. I assume that Julian is just peachy.

NORA. Why would you assume that?

LEE. Because if he weren't, we wouldn't be on our way to see half a play.

(relenting)

Fine, fine, fine, give me an update. Give me the daily, hourly Julian Report.

NORA. The doctors are releasing him tomorrow.

LEE. Really? When did he have his thingie?

NORA. Two weeks ago. And are you ever going to get over your talent for denial? What Julian had was not a "thingie." What Julian had was a stroke. A mini-stroke, to be exact.

LEE. Two weeks for - *(finding the courage to say it)* - A stroke is pretty good, isn't it?

NORA. He said he's not really a hundred percent yet.

LEE. When a doctor tells you can go, you get the hell outta there. They kept Hal Kramer at Cedars way longer than they should have after his prostate, you know, cancer thingie.

NORA. Don't remind me. I remember.

LEE. What an oozing, dripping mess that mistake was.

NORA. Thank you.

LEE. His legs got so rubbery, he kept plopping to the floor. The man was like an old cucumber when they buried him. He died like a Russian side dish.

NORA. Stop dwelling on it!

LEE. Make up your mind. You can have dwelling or you can have denying, all I'm saying's Julian's much better off in his condo than he is lying around at Cedars.

NORA. To his condo? In the shape that he's in? Are you serious?

LEE. Why? Is it some kind of Eskimo association where if you get old and sick they send you out on the ice?

NORA. You've been to his place.

LEE. Never had the pleasure.

NORA. It's like a tomb. He hasn't got one single window that faces the sun.

LEE. So, why can't he stay with Billy and Barbara?

NORA. Like they've suddenly got the room? And with the boys going through their wild Indian phase?

LEE. I find it hard to believe that Billy can't somehow accommodate his own father.

NORA. In the middle of the remodeling job they're in the middle of? Which, incidentally, I told him we're going to help out on some of the overruns.

LEE. I was wondering when that topic was going to stop hiding in the bushes. Which I got the bill for yesterday.

NORA. *(sailing on)* Somehow, I don't think Julian living in the middle of a construction site is exactly what the doctors had in mind for him.

*(**LEE**'s tie ends as close to even as he can manage:)*

LEE. Can we finally go? Please?

NORA. You know what I was thinking?

LEE. That would certainly be a first.

NORA. *(a beat, then)* I was thinking he could stay with us.

LEE. Who? Julian?

NORA. Julian.

LEE. We would have him stay with us?

NORA. That's right.

LEE. Which car were you thinking he'd sleep in?

NORA. Don't be silly.

LEE. You first, okay? Where could he possibly stay?

NORA. When's the last time you used the game room you just had to have so badly I fixed it up for you? A couple of coats of paint and we could turn that into a doll of a guest room.

LEE. (*flippantly*) Billy's contractor could probably do it in a couple of hours.

NORA. Three. He gave me an estimate.

LEE. No way, Nora. Forget it.

NORA. It'd only be for a couple of weeks, babe. That's all Julian needs.

LEE. He told you that?

NORA. His doctors did.

LEE. You talked with Julian's doctors?

NORA. Last week.

LEE. Last week? How long have you been consulting on this case?

NORA. From the day he went into Cedars. Billy wasn't visiting him as often as he could have, which is fine, Billy being Billy, but somebody had to take charge.

LEE. And you didn't say one word to me?

NORA. I didn't want to disturb you.

LEE. But it's okay to do it now?

(*after a beat*)

Nora, not only do I have to finish the new piece I just got that grant for, I have to score two pictures, both at the same time.

NORA. You'll just do what you have to do, that's all. You always do.

LEE. (*a deepening frown*) There's always, and then there's always.

NORA. Sweetheart, where else in the world can Julian turn to for the kind of hand God forbid anyone should ever find themselves in need of?

LEE. You don't owe him this. I certainly don't.

NORA. There's no owing anyone anything. A decent act doesn't need an excuse.

(a beat, then)

We're only talking a few weeks here. Then, he's willing to sell his condo and move into that new assisted living place in Santa Monica.

LEE. What new assisted living place?

NORA. It used to be Charles Laughton's estate. They call it The Bounty House. Penny Siegal did the interiors. She did a beautiful job.

LEE. You've been there?

NORA. Was I just gonna dump him somewhere sight unseen? Peggy gave Billy and me a tour.

LEE. Are you also taking flying lessons, running for president, or building an ark? What else is going on that I'm totally clueless about?

NORA. I just thought our house could serve as kind of an airlock while Julian recuperates.

LEE. An airlock. I'll be emptying bedpans in an airlock.

NORA. You won't have to empty anything. He'll have a professional caregiver.

LEE. And this bedpan engineer will be provided by –

NORA. An agency.

LEE. With whom you've already made the arrangements?

NORA. With whom I've been in preliminary contact. If a thing's worth doing, it's worth doing well, isn't that what you always say?

LEE. And just who is going to pay for all these well-done deeds?

NORA. Well, <u>we're</u> certainly gonna help out however we can, aren't we?

LEE. I guess we certainly are. Quite clearly, we're going to, but am I mistaken or isn't Julian a wealthy man?

NORA. Nobody's wealthy anymore.

LEE. That, I know. I was one of the pioneers of that movement.

NORA. This is a conversation we can have when we have it - number one, for a start, is getting him settled in.

LEE. No matter how it may upset the order of life as we know it.

NORA. *(perfecting his imperfect tie knot)* Lee...put yourself in his place!

LEE. You're asking if he can be in my place, why would I put myself in his?

(A beat; then, finally, with a sigh)

Okay, okay, okay! Julian can come stay with us.

NORA. *(terrifically pleased)* Thank you, sweetheart.

LEE. But only because he's your ex-husband.

(Lights fade, as THEY start to exit. The first, tentative bars of what LEE is composing are heard on a piano.)

Scene Two

(Daytime)

(The living room of Julian's Santa Monica condo.)

(Stairs lead to a second floor. **NORA** *is with her son,* **BILLY**. **BILLY** *holds an archive box.)*

NORA. *(consulting her list)* While you're in the bedroom, bring down your father's robe. The tartan.

BILLY. The plaid one?

NORA. *(patiently)* Yes, Billy. His plaid tartan. It's on his hassock. His hassock footstool. And collect whatever he's got on top of his nightstand, book-wise.

BILLY. Right.

NORA. Especially all of his Reader's Digests. And his Magic Markers and his Post-Its.

BILLY. What about his DVDs? He really enjoyed the Holocaust I gave him last Christmas.

NORA. Leave 'em. He said had enough TV in the hospital. The truth is, he falls asleep anyway. Even before his stroke. He hasn't seen the last hour and a half of anything in years.

BILLY. What else up there?

NORA. *(looking at her list)* His navy blue track suit. Look on the back of the chairs. To your father, every chair has become a closet.

BILLY. *(somewhat scattered)* The blue one with the white stripes?

NORA. He looks very handsome in it. Anything blue, in fact.

(off **BILLY** *'s look)*

Your father's always been an extremely attractive man.

BILLY. ...Mom?

*(**NORA** is busy checking her list.)*

Is Lee really okay with this? With Pop moving in with you guys?

NORA. A hundred percent.

BILLY. You sure?

NORA. Your father made that an absolute condition. Lee had to give his okay or there was no way he would consider living with us. If there's one thing Julian Cowan is a stubborn mule about, it's his pride.

BILLY. Lee's a lot less easy-going than he looks, you know. He's one of those quiet steamers.

NORA. Your stepfather has a very big heart. He knows this is the right thing to do.

BILLY. You know what he said? He said you were taking Dad in because of your guilt.

NORA. Lee said that?

BILLY. Because, you know - because of you leaving Pop for him.

NORA. As right as he can be, that's how wrong he is. I left your father for me, not for anybody else. Can someone only do a good deed because someone else thinks you did a bad one, which I'm not for one minute saying my leaving your father was?

BILLY. Do you still love him at all?

NORA. Who're we talking about? Your father? Julian?

BILLY. Even a little?

NORA. No, not romantically, I don't. But I'll always love that time when I did. A divorce is not a lobotomy, Billy.

(consulting her list)

Don't forget his aftershave. I got Saks to order him some more.

BILLY. Right.

(He looks around the room.)

NORA. What?

BILLY. This place. I don't know if I should say it.

NORA. Say it.

BILLY. It's such a kind of a, I don't know.

NORA. A shithouse, right?

BILLY. It hurts me to see him living here.

NORA. That's why, starting tomorrow, he's not going to be here one day more.

BILLY. *(a beat, then)* Was it really that awful?

NORA. Transient ischemic, according to your father's heart man. He said, if you're going to have one, it's the Rolls-Royce of strokes.

BILLY. I mean being married to Pop.

NORA. What happened happened, Billy. There's a reason it's called the past, you know.

BILLY. Right.

> *(taking the list from her)*

I'll be back down in a day or two.

NORA. *(apologetically)* I know it's a lot. I want him to feel at home.

> (**BILLY** *starts up the stairs.*)

Billy?

BILLY. *(stopping, testily)* What? You want me to bring down his bathtub? His toilet seat? What??

NORA. There's no need for that.

BILLY. Sorry.

> *(a beat, then)*

I am. What?

NORA. I just wanna say, Friday night, after they let your father go, why don't you and Barbara come to the house for dinner? The boys, too, if they can use each other as punching bags for five minutes.

BILLY. Fine. Good. We'll come.

> *(a beat, then)*

It'll probably be just me, though.

NORA. Bring everybody. A little ruckus'll pep him up.

> *(off his nervous tugging at a lock of his hair)*

Why're you doing that again?

BILLY. What?

NORA. *(miming him)* That nervous thing you used to do with your hair.

BILLY. *(lying)* I didn't get a lotta sleep last night.

NORA. *(not buying it)* Billy? The truth?

    (After a long moment:)

BILLY. *(blurting it out)* Barbara's having an affair.

NORA. Get out of here!

BILLY. She is! I saw her, Mom!

NORA. You couldn't have!

BILLY. I saw them both!

NORA. You saw Barbara and someone together?

BILLY. I sure as hell did!

NORA. What, having coffee, that kind of thing?

BILLY. No, Mom. Having sex, <u>that</u> kind of thing!

NORA. Sex? You're sure that's what they were doing?

BILLY. …What else looks like that?

NORA. That is sickening!

BILLY. Trust me, they didn't seem to think so.

NORA. Where were they doing it? Where did this happen?

BILLY. On the floor.

NORA. On the floor?

BILLY. On the floor.

NORA. On what floor?

BILLY. On the floor in our den!

NORA. In your den - in your own house?

BILLY. That's right.

NORA. They were on the floor? And they were doing it to each other?

BILLY. Screwing each other's brains out.

NORA. On the Berber?!

BILLY. On the Berber!

NORA. That's disgusting!

BILLY. You think?!

NORA. That carpeting was a wedding present from me and Lee!

BILLY. Well, she's getting a lot of enjoyment out of it.

(*twisting a lock of his hair again*)

Loads.

NORA. What happened? What did she say?

BILLY. All I heard was her moaning.

NORA. I mean, when you told her you saw her.

BILLY. I haven't told her I did.

NORA. What're you talking about? You didn't talk to her?

BILLY. No.

NORA. (*re his fooling with his hair*) Stop that!

(*HE does.*)

NORA. How can you not have said something? Anything?

BILLY. I don't know if I could without throwing up.

NORA. Have you told your father?

BILLY. It only happened yesterday.

NORA. Take my advice: don't! His heart's on one leg as it is. He doesn't need this kind of news now.

BILLY. I'd appreciate it if you didn't tell Lee either.

NORA. Lee? Why?

BILLY. He always told me that sooner or later Barbara would do this kind of thing. I don't want to give him the satisfaction.

NORA. Lee said Barbara would cheat on you?

BILLY. More than once.

NORA. Where would he get that idea?

BILLY. I don't know. He said he knew the look.

NORA. I'm sure he does.

BILLY. Meaning?

NORA. Meaning never mind.

(*a beat, then*)

How did you catch 'em at it? Did you just happen to walk in and surprise 'em?

BILLY. Yesterday, I got a lift home from work 'cause my car's still in the shop. I'm not two steps into the front hall, and there they are, big as life, going to town all over the closed circuit.

NORA. On the closed circuit?

BILLY. That's right.

NORA. Since when do you have closed circuit?

BILLY. Barbara decided to install it. For security. It's part of the remodeling.

NORA. You never told me you were doing that.

BILLY. He only just put it in last week.

NORA. Who put it in?

BILLY. The guy who's been putting it into Barbara!

NORA. *(comes the dawn)* She's having an affair with the contractor?

BILLY. Can you believe it?

NORA. How long has this been going on?

BILLY. Months.

NORA. Months?

BILLY. He's a contractor!

NORA. So now?

BILLY. So now what now?

NORA. Tell me what you're gonna do about it!

BILLY. I don't know.

(a beat, then)

Nothing, I guess.

NORA. Nothing? That's your master plan? Nothing?

BILLY. I'm going to let it run its course, what else can I do?

NORA. The woman's ass is covered in rug burns, there's omelet all over your face, and you're gonna just let it run its course?

BILLY. You want me to get down on my knees? You want me to beg her to stop? No way! Forget it!

NORA. Stop yelling at your mother!

BILLY. I'm sorry!

NORA. I'm not the one who's spread out all over the Berber, Billy!

BILLY. I said I'm sorry!

NORA. (*a beat; then, calmly*) All right, now, let's work this out, step by step.

BILLY. Like how?

NORA. The first thing is, you talk to her.

BILLY. Never!

(*after a beat*)

And say what?

NORA. For openers, she's gotta know that you know. You've gotta find out for sure how long she and this rat've been - keeping company. For all you know, that floor business could've been a one-shot thing.

BILLY. Not from the way they were going at it.

NORA. Okay, okay. Then, you've gotta get tough. You have to really lay it on her. You have to tell her you're both going to start getting counseling.

BILLY. No, sir! I'm not starting up with a counselor.

NORA. Everybody sees one sooner or later.

BILLY. Never again! I still remember that guy in the Valley you sent me to when you and Dad broke up, the one with the gross breath and the Disney action figures.

NORA. He was a child psychologist. You're not going this time because someone tried to touch your pee-pee.

BILLY. I'm not doing it! I can handle this myself.

NORA. To save your marriage, you won't try it just once?

BILLY. So I can sit there and listen to everything I've done wrong?

NORA. Who says you've done anything wrong?

BILLY. Barbara will. She'll say I'm not romantic. She'll say I don't want it enough. She'll say I want it too often. She'll make me sound like I'm two different people than who I am!

NORA. You let this fester, it'll eat you alive.

BILLY. I am not going to have that conversation! I don't even want to have this one!

NORA. Your marriage means nothing at all to you, is that what you're saying?

BILLY. My marriage means everything to me! That's why I'm not going to cut it open with a friggin' chain-saw and make it run around somebody's office with its guts falling out! I didn't talk to you about what's going on in my life so you could send me to see someone I could talk about it to. I just wanted a little sympathy, that's all.

NORA. That you've always got, you know that. But think, sweetheart: if you do nothing but let this thing run its course - it might just run its course right out the front door. And with all its bags packed.

BILLY. Like you did?

NORA. I'm not on trial here! Maybe in Lee's mind I am, but I certainly am not in my own!

BILLY. You went your separate way, I'll go <u>my</u> separate way.

NORA. And the boys?

BILLY. This boy turned out just fine.

NORA. In that if you're not careful you're gonna wind up looking like a plucked chicken?

(a beat, then)

Face this, Billy. Don't bury it. You go home and you talk to her.

BILLY. What if she doesn't want to?

NORA. Ask her again. Let her know you at least <u>tried</u> to turn things around. That you think she's valuable enough to hold onto forever.

(a pause, then)

Darling boy? For me?

(A long moment passes.)

BILLY. All right. Okay.

NORA. Better, right?

>*(pleased, her arms around him)*

>Rest. Relax.

BILLY. Good luck.

NORA. *(spotting an object)* Oh. Don't forget to take Dad's album.

BILLY. I will.

>(**NORA** *picks up the cracked leather album and opens it.*)

>(**BILLY** *retrieves an old snapshot that falls out of its pages. Re picture:*)

BILLY. Pop took that.

NORA. I know.

BILLY. That's the pony that threw me.

NORA. I remember.

BILLY. What was I, like four years old?

NORA. Uh huh.

>*(studying the snapshot)*

>I hope they made glue out of the dirty little bastard.

>*(As **BILLY** boxes the album, the lights fade.)*

>*(A more developed version of Lee's composition is heard.)*

Scene Three

(Afternoon.)

(LEE, *in bright, Hawaiian shirt, jeans and loafers, "drives" an "SUV.")*

(His frail backseat passenger is **JULIAN COWAN.***)*

(Dressed for the arctic, **JULIAN** *will occasionally drink from a large sippy cup.)*

(After a long, long beat:)

LEE. How you doing back there?

JULIAN. *(not really)* Terrific.

(a beat, then)

Best day of my life.

LEE. *(another long beat, trying for affability)* It never fails how you can't see the hills sometimes, you know? Bigger than life, and we can't see them for all the sludge up there. When I first moved to L.A.? When the West Coast was still like a secret? Every day was crystal-like. Restaurants gave away free orange juice, they were so anxious to get rid of all the goddamn things.

JULIAN. *(a beat, then)* Can I tell you something?

LEE. Of course, Julian.

JULIAN. We don't need to talk.

LEE. It's strictly your call.

JULIAN. I don't say that to be rude.

LEE. Hey, you don't want to talk, you don't want to talk.

JULIAN. All I'm saying is we don't have to make conversation.

LEE. Gotcha. The next sound you hear from me will be total silence.

JULIAN. Don't take it wrong. I appreciate all this immensely, your letting me stay with you, etcetera.

LEE. I'm sure you'd do the same if it were the other way around.

JULIAN. I'm sure I would, too, because Nora would make me. Just like she's making you.

LEE. That's not true.

JULIAN. Did she tell you I told her in no uncertain terms she <u>had</u> to ask you? That she had to give you every opportunity to say no?

LEE. I was given every opportunity to do that.

JULIAN. We were married a long time. I know how things go with her. I made it very clear that going back to the condo wouldn't faze me one iota.

LEE. There's no need to do that, Julian, absolutely none!

JULIAN. Good.

> *(The sound of* **LEE**'s *cell phone is heard coming from his pocket. As* **LEE** *fishes it out:)*

> On the subject of talking, the last thing we need is a lot of pointless chit-chat, pretending what's happening's some kind of fun for either one of us.

LEE. *(re cell phone)* Let me get this.

> *(into the cell)*

> Hey!

> *(Light rise on* **NORA** *on a treadmill stage left.)*

NORA. *(on her cell phone)* Did you get our boy?

LEE. Got him right here. I'll put you on speaker.

> *(***LEE** *"does" so.)*

NORA. Julian? It's Nora.

JULIAN. *(suddenly weaker)* Hello, Nora.

NORA. Are you all right?

> *(seeking confirmation)*

> Lee?

LEE. I'd say he's ready to go ten rounds with anyone.

NORA. Are you warm enough, Julian?

JULIAN. *(unconvincingly)* I'm okay.

NORA. Put the heater on, Lee. The last thing he needs is a chill now.

LEE. Nora, it's 86 degrees outside.

NORA. Lee?

LEE. I'm doing it, I'm doing it. You two let me know if you want it any warmer, I'll set the car on fire.

NORA. Listen to me, sweetheart.

BOTH. *(in unison)* What?

NORA. I was talking to Julian.

LEE. Pardon me.

NORA. I'm sorry about not picking you up at the hospital. I forgot about the conflict with my personal trainer.

JULIAN. I understand.

NORA. Before I call the bed place, I wanna make sure they're gonna send the right one over. Have you decided between the Sealy and the Tempur-pedic?

JULIAN. Go with the Sealy. It's good enough.

NORA. You said the Tempur-pedic was the top of the line.

JULIAN. I'm not looking to spend a fortune. Nora. The Tempurpedic's like a thousand more. I'm not spending that much money just to be unconscious on!

NORA. Don't concern yourself. The bed'll be our gift to you, right, Lee?

LEE. *(optionless)* Right.

JULIAN. *(aside, to LEE)* This is not a good start.

LEE. It'll be fine.

NORA. If you're going to have a stroke, you're not gonna go tourist, Julian. And, Lee?

LEE. Yes?

NORA. Remember what I told you about not taking the freeway!

LEE. I remember.

NORA. I'll see you both when you get here, okay? You boys stay out of trouble.

*(The light fades on **NORA**.)*

JULIAN. *(a beat, then)* I'm going to pay you back, you know. For everything.

LEE. You don't have to, Julian.

JULIAN. I do, Lee. And I will.

LEE. She won't let you, you know that. But thank you for offering.

(After another long moment:)

JULIAN. You like this gas guzzler?

LEE. I thought no small talk?

JULIAN. Cars are my business.

(corrects himself)

<u>Were</u> my business, before my heart joined up for the ischemic club. Billy gave you a good deal on your lease, right? I'm not making dime one on this one.

LEE. Much appreciated, Julian.

(After a beat, LEE *"turns the wheel.")*

LEE. Do me a favor? Don't tell Nora I took the freeway.

JULIAN. Why would I?

(a beat, then)

Nora still handles all the car stuff for you two?

LEE. The car, the house, our taxes. I'm in charge of the   • piano, she's in charge of the world.

JULIAN. It suits you, though, right?

LEE. It's fine. I can't tell you the last time I felt like a grown-up, though.

JULIAN. Maybe you should just shut up and count your blessings.

LEE. *(a little annoyed)* Okay.

JULIAN. Believe me, the alternative is pretty miserable.

LEE. *(coolly)* Thanks for the reminder.

JULIAN. *(after a long moment)* I'm probably gonna give my Buick to Billy.

LEE. Why don't you wait awhile, see how you feel?

JULIAN. I was thinking in the hospital. Whether I get better or I don't, either way, there comes a time you turn off the car key in your head. How many people'd that old guy run over last year in Santa Monica, up to his ass on God knows how many meds?

LEE. He killed as many as he could, I guess.

JULIAN. Sixty years I've been driving. What's sixty times, say, ten thousand miles a year? Must be like almost a million.

LEE. It's a long trip.

JULIAN. I must be there by now, huh? Wherever I was going?

LEE. *(a beat, then)* How 'bout some music?

JULIAN. *(not interested)* I'm good. Nora tells me you got a commission to write something on your own?

LEE. If I ever get past bar twelve, I will.

JULIAN. What is it? Some kind of a concerto like?

LEE. It's an elegy, actually.

JULIAN. Anybody I knew?

LEE. No, no, it's kind of a generic dirge. Every time I turn around these days, I find myself speaking at the funeral du jour.

JULIAN. Lately, it's like they started giving death away for free.

LEE. *(agreeing)* Y'know? I thought I'd write a piece of music instead of just getting up and making one more speech. Words don't seem to cut it anymore. If, in fact, they ever did.

JULIAN. That's some talent, y'know? Hearing all that stuff in your head that no one else does.

LEE. In some places, it's called insanity.

JULIAN. As long as it pays well, right?

LEE. I guess. What can I say? I've been lucky.

JULIAN. You've been very lucky. Very. But you also went out and took what you wanted. You still do. That's a very efficient combination.

(LEE's *cell phone warbles again. As* LEE *picks it up:*)

LEE. (*to* JULIAN) I guess I'll take that as a compliment?

JULIAN. I never had a tenth of your moxie. If I did, I'd probably still be married to Nora.

LEE. (*uncomfortably*) Julian...

JULIAN. Answer the phone.

LEE. (*gruffly, into his cell*) What do <u>you</u> want?

(*A light rises on* NORA, *astride a stationary bike stage right, her cell phone to her ear.*)

NORA. What kind of way is that to answer a phone?

(*imitating him*)

"What do <u>you</u> want?"

LEE. I'm sorry! What do you want, <u>darling?</u>

NORA. Put me on speaker.

LEE. (*aside, to* JULIAN) It's the mothership.

(LEE *switches* NORA's *call to the car's speaker-phone.*)

NORA. Julian?

JULIAN. I'm as warm as a bug in a rug.

NORA. I know how concerned you are about expenses so I want to check with you before I pull the trigger with the nursing agency.

JULIAN. And?

NORA. I've interviewed a few girls, and the one I think you should go with for the daytime is called Lotis. That's Lotis with an "I."

JULIAN. Never mind the spelling lesson, what does she get?

NORA. One twenty.

JULIAN. (*pained*) For the day?

NORA. One twenty an <u>hour</u>.

JULIAN. What're you, crazy?

NORA. (*overlapping his comment*) She's worth every penny. She's got a lovely disposition.

JULIAN. Wouldn't we all, at those prices?

NORA. *(pedals a bit, then)* …You're going to need one for the night, too, you know.

JULIAN. I have to pay to watch someone fall asleep before I do?

NORA. I talked to one woman who comes highly recommended.

JULIAN. By who? By Lotis, with an "I?" What does she charge, the night girl, if the day one gets one-twenty? Forget I even asked.

NORA. Two hundred's the going rate.

JULIAN. *(to LEE)* Take the airport exit. It's cheaper to drive to Lourdes.

NORA. *(stops pedaling)* The exit? The exit?

LEE. *(sotto voce, angrily)* What the hell, Julian?

JULIAN. *(sotto voce)* Sorry.

NORA. Lee? Didn't I tell you about the freeway? Especially after three in the afternoon?

LEE. The surface streets were jammed! I've been in the right lane the whole time!

JULIAN. *(helpfully)* He's driving like a soldier.

NORA. My God. You be careful with him, Lee. You hear me?

LEE. Christ, it's not like I'm bringing a baby home.

JULIAN. *(after a sip from his sippy cup)* A little, maybe.

NORA. *(toweling off)* Don't think we're not going to have a little talk about this freeway business.

LEE. I'd bet the car on that.

NORA. *(back to business)* What I suggest we do, Julian, is we go with Lotis for the daytime, and hire the registered nurse to stay with you through the night.

JULIAN. Absolutely not!

NORA. If you can't afford it, and you and I both know you can't, Lee and I'll help out until you get rid of the condo.

LEE. Is there a card I can sign to go with all these gifts?

JULIAN. Nora, I am not some kind of charity case!

NORA. Compassion is not charity.

JULIAN. Tell that to cash. Cash doesn't know the difference.

NORA. *(continuing her thought)* Compassion for someone I'll always care about.

LEE. *(aside, to* JULIAN*)* I see this scene with violins.

NORA. You got anyone else that can help you at this point in your life, Julian?

JULIAN. It wasn't my idea to outlive everyone I knew.

NORA. Look, we don't have to solve what're not even really problems yet all in one call.

LEE. Who can keep track anymore?

NORA. Was that you, Lee?

LEE. I forgot we're still on the air.

NORA. How many times have I told you? Stay off the phone when you're on the freeway!

(She hangs up.)

(Lights down on NORA.*)*

(A moment passes; then:)

JULIAN. He never saw it coming.

LEE. Who's that?

JULIAN. This *Reader's Digest* story where a guy got hit by a bus. That was the title.

LEE. "He Never Saw it Coming?"

JULIAN. That's right. He was walking alone at night down a highway. He was minding his own business, he wasn't looking for trouble, he was just walking along with an iThing in his ear.

LEE. *(helpfully)* An iPod.

JULIAN. I said that.

(a beat, then)

It's pitch as black can be outside. The road is icy. By the time the bus driver made him out, the poor bastard'd already lost one arm and both of his legs. He dove right into therapy though. Now, he's teaching chess to the same inner city kids that were on the bus that hit him.

(a beat, then)

JULIAN. It got me really thinking, that story.

LEE. Oh?

JULIAN. It got me thinking what were you thinking that night?

LEE. The night the guy got hit by a bus?

JULIAN. If you even were thinking at all.

LEE. Wait a minute. What are we suddenly talking about here?

JULIAN. You meet a woman at a party. An unattached woman, except she's got on a wedding ring, which you either ignore, or worse, you don't give a good goddam about. Or worse than worse, you figure that makes her some kind of a door prize.

LEE. Julian, after so many years of avoiding this conversation - after all the times you've come to dinner, shared birthdays and Billy's Little League games with us, why are you suddenly bringing this subject so completely out of the blue right now?

JULIAN. Because it's important that we finally talk about it.

LEE. Who says?

JULIAN. The injured party says, that's who!

LEE. *(heatedly)* Excuse me, but maybe you should have filed a complaint at the time, sir!

JULIAN. I didn't just think about Buicks and car keys in the hospital, all right? Like it or lump it, you and I are going to have a talk about what I want to talk about even before we get to your house!

LEE. And I'm telling you that if we do have it, we might never get to the goddam house!

JULIAN. *(overlapping the above)* I just need to understand how you saw the situation!

LEE. *(continuing, overlapping the above)* Because I'm gonna pull over and first kill you and then myself with a tire iron!

JULIAN. Just for once, finally explain to me why you had absolutely no regard for what I might have felt about what was going on without me having so much as one stinking inkling about it! I accept that you had no regard for me! I understand that it was so much easier stealing someone from someone you didn't even know! But what about Nora? She was a married woman, for God's sake! A married woman with a child, which you soon enough found out about! Did you ever once give as much as a hoot about anyone else just as long as you got whatever - or whoever - you wanted?

LEE. I didn't walk up to her with a plan, Julian! I didn't wake up that morning with the idea that that was the day I was going to change my whole life!

JULIAN. How about three whole lives?!

LEE. All it started out as was a simple conversation at a party.

JULIAN. But you pushed it! Just tell me if you were thinking you were doing the right thing when you pushed it!

LEE. I wasn't thinking, Julian, I was falling in love!

JULIAN. But I fell in love with her first!

(**LEE**'s cell phone rings.)

(**LEE** answers.)

(Both men, both irritated, respond.)

LEE & JULIAN. WHAT?!

(Blackout)

(In the darkness, we hear Lee's elegy played at its next stage of development.)

Scene Four

(The Baers' morning room.)

(A casually dressed **LEE** *is playing gin rummy with* **JULIAN**.*)*

(An old, plaid robe over his pajamas, **JULIAN** *'s garb is topped by a jaunty, paisley ascot, as much for the touch of flair it lends as the warmth that it provides.)*

(After drawing a fresh card from the center pile and giving his next move a moment of thought:)

LEE. *(nervously)* It may be a little late, but –

(laying the cards in his hands down)

Six.

(a beat, then)

Any good?

(turning his face-down knock card right-side up)

That's the Jack you've been waiting for, right?

(getting no response)

The Jack of Hearts?

(stares at **JULIAN***; then, to himself)*

Jesus.

(clinking **JULIAN'***s teacup with a spoon)*

Julian?

(more clinking, then)

Julian!

JULIAN. *(coming to, disoriented)* What?
LEE. Are you all right?

(As **JULIAN** *reaches toward the center pile:)*

No! Don't!

JULIAN. *(startled)* What?!

   (trying to remember)

   You just discarded, didn't you?

LEE. I just knocked.

JULIAN. With how much?

LEE. Six points.

   (hopefully)

   Am I okay?

JULIAN. *(looking at* **LEE**'s *face-up knock card)*
Is that the Jack of Hearts?

LEE. It's the card you needed, right?

JULIAN. Not any more I don't!

   (He snaps up the Jack gleefully.)

   (Using one triumphant elbow, **JULIAN** *inserts the Jack into his cards, and declares:)*

   Gin!

   (He lays down what he thinks is his winning hand.)

LEE. You can't do that.

   (JULIAN *cackles.)*

   You can't gin after someone knocks.

JULIAN. Who knocked?

LEE. I did.

JULIAN. When?

LEE. When you fell asleep.

JULIAN. Never! I didn't!

LEE. I saw you!

JULIAN. I was resting. I was waiting for you to make up your mind.

LEE. I <u>did</u> make up my mind. I went down with six. You got less than that?

JULIAN. You caught me with a million points, but I'd've ginned, if you'd have given me the chance.

LEE. Close only counts in horseshoes.

JULIAN. *(testy)* Whatever you say, Tom.

LEE. *(puzzled)* Tom?

JULIAN. Tom Mix. Horseshoes. You're a maven on those, too, now?

LEE. *(keeping his cool)* How about we just pack it in for while, all right, Julian?

JULIAN. It's your bunkhouse. You call the shots. I was only playing to please you.

LEE. *(gathering up the cards)* I think I've had more than enough pleasure for one day.

JULIAN. *(truculently)* Fine.

LEE. Same time tomorrow?

JULIAN. *(the same)* Fine.

LEE. Right. Same time, same place.

(under his breath, wearily)

Or else at Guantanamo.

JULIAN. What'd you say?

LEE. I said "Same time, same place."

JULIAN. I heard that part. I meant when you said, "Or else at Guantanamo."

LEE. *(re-boxing the deck)* For someone who doesn't hear well, you could give hearing lessons.

(offering **JULIAN** *the remote channel changer)*

You want to watch some Wimbledon if it's on?

JULIAN. *(refusing the remote)* They play whether I watch them or not.

(a beat, then)

Tell me something.

LEE. *(bracing himself)* What's that?

JULIAN. Are you as tired as you look lately?

LEE. A little, maybe. Could be.

JULIAN. *(after a beat)* Around three this morning, I could hear you playing the piano.

LEE. It kind of goes with the territory around here.

JULIAN. Was what I heard you playing the thing you're writing?

LEE. The thing I <u>thought</u> I could, yes.

JULIAN. The little I heard sounds like it would go over very big at a funeral.

LEE. I'm sorry if I woke you.

JULIAN. *(with a shrug)* Everything wakes me. <u>Sleeping</u> wakes me. That goes with another kind of territory.

(a beat, then)

Can I tell you what I thought about what I did hear, for whatever it's worth?

LEE. *(automatically defensive)* It's not finished yet.

JULIAN. *(barging ahead)* Sometimes, in places, the melody, you probably call it, it goes up when I thought it was going to go down. Sometimes I just didn't know where it was going altogether. I never knew what to expect.

LEE. It's called the element of surprise, Julian. It's not unlike life itself.

JULIAN. Only when you make something up, you decide what's in, you decide what's out. <u>You</u> get to be God, right?

LEE. Until I have to take a leak, I am.

JULIAN. *(off* LEE *sneaking a look at his wrist watch)* Did Nora tell you?

LEE. That depends on what, but the answer is probably no.

JULIAN. I got a call from Sonia today.

LEE. *(instant interest)* The real estate Sonia?

JULIAN. She just got another offer on my condo.

LEE. Another <u>tentative</u> offer?

JULIAN. Better than that, she said. The Russians want to take a second look.

LEE. *(most interested)* They do? Really?

JULIAN. Maybe this time, huh? Maybe, maybe?

LEE. I'm keeping everything crossed for you, Julian, I really am.

JULIAN. *(understanding the reference)* I had no idea I was going to be with you this long, you know. Not in my wildest dreams. What's it been? Almost six weeks now?

LEE. More like ten weeks tomorrow, if you care to be exact.

JULIAN. *(surprised)* Ten weeks! No way!

LEE. You and I have talked about this several times before, Julian.

JULIAN. *(puzzled)* We have?

LEE. We've had this entire conversation. Word for word.

JULIAN. You know my number one rule of thumb? Any conversation I don't remember, I never had in the first place.

LEE. That's a terrific rule.

JULIAN. Had it or not, that's how you must feel by now, about my being with you.

LEE. However I feel, we made a deal, Julian.

JULIAN. This is not some kind of nice contest. A deal is a deal but temporary is also temporary. I'm getting out of your hair just as soon as I can get rid of that millstone of a condo.

LEE. I know you will.

JULIAN. *(suddenly weary)* What does your watch say?

LEE. *(checking)* Ten to noon. Nap time?

JULIAN. It's not a matter of choice. You don't need me in your face wherever you look anyway.

LEE. I might just try to get some work done.

JULIAN. At home or will you drive to the studio?

LEE. I've got a ton of stuff I'm behind on wherever I do it.

JULIAN. One favor, Lee, if you don't leave the house?

(a beat, then)

If you wouldn't mind? I'd really appreciate it if you didn't play the piano.

LEE. *(taken aback)* Not play the piano? While I'm composing?

JULIAN. Is that a problem? Beethoven was deaf, you know.

LEE. And Tchaikovsky was gay. So?

JULIAN. I was thinking especially if you're going to do any work on your elegy.

LEE. That piece bothers you?

JULIAN. It's not only that it keeps going up where I think it's going to go down.

LEE. *(the silent steamer)* It's all those other pesky little notes?

JULIAN. It's an elegy. Lee. I hardly need the reminder.

LEE. Gotcha. I'll work on something else.

JULIAN. *(putting on his Jackie O sunglasses)* That is one bright sun today.

LEE. *(still processing Julian's request)* It is, indeed.

JULIAN. *(ready to go)* Goodnight, Lee.

LEE. Goodnight, Julian.

(The lights fade.)

(For the first time, we hear no piano whatsoever in the darkness between scenes.)

Scene Five

(Late morning.)

(The Baers' Beverly Hills driveway.)

(**NORA** *stands waiting, looking at the o.s. house.*)

(**LEE** *paces.*)

(Both are dressed informally.)

LEE. You know, I came home early from the studio especially.

NORA. *(uncomfortably)* I know.

LEE. I was really cooking. I looked up at the clock. I quit, like I promised to, and now, here we are. Nowhere. Nowhere we're supposed to be. Just you and me, stuck in the middle of downtown limbo.

NORA. *(after a beat)* I'll go in and get him.

LEE. You stay right there.

(opening a bag of M&M's)

Let's let Mohammed come down from the second floor for a change.

NORA. *(antsy)* This is not like him.

LEE. He's probably falling down somewhere. The man's gotta get his exercise, you know.

NORA. That's cruel.

LEE. So's wasting other people's time.

(**NORA** *watches* **LEE** *stuff his face with the candy.*)

NORA. Can't you put those in your mouth like a normal human being?

LEE. *(popping a few more into his mouth)* I'm hungry.

NORA. The Father's Day Special at the club is crab cakes. You're going to ruin your appetite.

LEE. My appetite for this farcical event was pre-ruined way before I opened this bag of chocolate rabbit poops.

NORA. *(after a long beat)* God. Sometimes I wonder –

LEE. *(quoting, not singing, the lyric)* "Why you spend the lonely nights?"

NORA. Why, of all the men in the world to pick me –

LEE. I never picked you, Nora. You were assigned to me by the gods so that you could teach me how to eat candy and how not to finish my work.

NORA. It's not my fault if you're stuck.

LEE. I am not stuck.

NORA. I know stuck when I hear it.

LEE. I told you, I was on a roll! The best in years!

NORA. How come it's only the good stuff that ever gets interrupted?

LEE. Because the bad shit doesn't need me. Bad shit writes itself.

(a beat, then)

What I <u>am</u> fighting, my dear, is the goddamned calendar, and whatever scraps are left of my former concentration, which has been completely shot to pieces, thanks to the half dozen daily dramas starring –

(louder, in the direction of the house)

– We both know exactly who!

NORA. *(confidentially)* You'll finish.

LEE. I don't know. For the first time in my life, I might just go belly-up at the keyboard. You let yourself get dragged far enough away from a piece, you can lose your way back. It happens.

NORA. You know, as frightfully important as your work is –

LEE. It's paid the bills for more years than I can remember. Has that been a problem for you? I didn't think so.

NORA. *(overlapping, continuing)* There are these little things in our lives that also require our attention called "people." They're not eighth notes, or triplets, or abstract ideas. They're real as hell, people are, and the only deadlines they really care about are their own, inasmuch as they sometimes get selfishly ill, thoughtlessly old, and they heal at the slow, cosmically insulting rate that they heal.

LEE. Or they don't. Sometimes they just settle in and get a little too used to being waited on hand and foot.

NORA. *(a beat, then)* I'm going inside.

(starting off)

Maybe Lotis can use a hand with him.

LEE. Lotis is more than capable at her job.

NORA. *(stopping)* She's from heaven, that woman. You ever seen her give Julian a bath?

LEE. I can't tell you how many times I've fought the urge to sneak in and watch.

NORA. The way she sponges him down. And oils him. So gentle, so caring.

LEE. It must be like working on the Dead Sea Scrolls.

NORA. Tell me you don't wish someone treated you like that.

LEE. I could have had a stroke. I turned it down.

NORA. *(freshly frustrated)* Why are you eating that trash when you know we're about to go have an actual meal?

LEE. Because so far, we're not. In all probability, we never will. We're going to stand out here for at least another hour. That hour will stretch into two. Tomorrow will be followed by tomorrow night. Then, weeks from now, this is where they'll find us: dead in our own driveway. Dead in our own Beverly Hills Donner Pass.

NORA. Oh, please.

LEE. *(ranting on)* And when the TV crews descend on the place to determine which one of us ate the other one first, Julian will -

(demonstrating)

- finally come walkering out the door on all six of his legs, like the tower of human Jell-O that he is.

NORA. *(after a beat)* Don't think he doesn't notice.

LEE. Doesn't notice what?

NORA. You don't think it's painfully obvious how you go out of your way to avoid him?

LEE. That's not true!

NORA. When was the last time you sat down with him and actually talked to him?

LEE. I talk to Julian all the time.

NORA. I don't mean rushing past him with a perfunctory "How ya doing," without even looking his way.

LEE. It's not perfunctory. I always make a point of feigning very deep interest.

NORA. Aside from a few half-hearted, half-finished gin games, when was the last time you asked him how he was doing and cared two cents worth whether you got an answer or not?

LEE. To tell you the God's honest truth, my dear, I haven't got some kind of built-in give-a-shit-ometer. I don't know!

NORA. Let me tell you then, okay? Never is <u>exactly</u> how often you've actually talked to him man to man, person to person, since the day he moved in with us.

LEE. Oh, I get it.

NORA. You get what?

LEE. I get that this is something Julian's whined to you about.

NORA. Unlike some people who I happen to be talking to at this very moment, Julian has never been a whiner.

LEE. <u>Ex</u>-love is also blind, right? Maybe a little deaf, too?

NORA. Nobody likes feeling like they're not really there!

LEE. Really? I never would have known!

NORA. *(lightly shocked)* <u>You're</u> feeling neglected?

LEE. Between you taking him on his trips to whole medical towers filled with more scanners than anyone's come up with diseases for, plus all the Memory Lane mileage you two pile up looking at his album filled with fading Polaroids? Just a little, Missus! Maybe just a little!

NORA. I can't believe this! Julian and I had once had a life together. We had a child together!

LEE. Oh, I know that child very well! I straightened that child's teeth! I paid through my <u>own</u> teeth to put that child's little ass on one private school bus after another all the years Julian never once kicked in whatever child support he was supposed to!

NORA. Is there any part of the past you're not above dredging up?

LEE. That's what pasts are for, my dear. It's pretty hard to dredge up the future, you know.

NORA. This is so entirely not the time for this kind of carping.

LEE. Tell me your hours, I can come back.

NORA. For God's sake, Lee. The man is sick!

LEE. Sick? "The man" is a walking, sneak preview of death! The chill of the grave rolls off him in waves!

NORA. I have to tell you, I never would have asked if he could stay with us. <u>Never!</u>

LEE. You "asked" me? The only reason you "asked" me was because you know I'm a complete and utter pushover for doing whatever it is you want me to.

NORA. Among the countless others too numerous to mention.

LEE. Don't open a second front on me, okay? If you'll recall, we talked about Julian being with us for just a little while. I'd say an eight month stay qualifies as just a little north of "little while" country, wouldn't you? There was also talk of an airlock, I believe. Or did I imagine that, too?

NORA. The idea that he's been with us anywhere near eight months is preposterous.

LEE. Oh? Are we on different calendars now?

(showing her the calendar on his cell phone)

Check it out. Tomorrow - and with my luck, there probably will be one - tomorrow will make exactly eight months since we began our little ménage-à-trois-in-the-ass!

NORA. *(amazed)* You've been counting the days?

LEE. Not at all. I stopped counting the days when they turned into weeks, and then into months, which, as of tomorrow, will be eight of the goddam things!

NORA. It's not Julian's fault there've been complications. Or mine either, for that matter.

LEE. Who said it was?!

NORA. We signed up to help the man get better!

LEE. Oh, don't taunt me with visions of that delicious, unattainable past tense! I cannot wait to look back fondly on all the colonoscopies, on all the PET and the CAT results, back to the glorious era when every breakfast, lunch and dinner was either devoted to a medical conference on urinary flow charts or a chance to mull over one more pathetically tentative offer on that infinitely unsellable condo of his! Just think! These tortuous moments will turn out to be the good old days! And me, like an idiot, I'm taking them all for granted!

NORA. You know what?

LEE. Probably not, what?

NORA. If it's so hard for you to deal with the fact that someone else's needs supersede your own for a few short months, why don't you just go cry on what's-her-face's shoulder for awhile?

LEE. If you're talking about Marla –

NORA. Keep your voice down.

LEE. Oh? Afraid my ex-husband-in-law will hear?

NORA. If he hasn't already.

LEE. You didn't tell him?

NORA. I've had all the embarrassment I can handle, thank you.

LEE. The truth is, I <u>would</u> consider talking to her if I could, but as it turns out, she's out of town.

NORA. *(threatened)* How do you know?

LEE. I read it on the front page of the Entertainment section in the effing *L.A. Times*, would you kindly lose the panicked tone?

NORA. What'd it say?

LEE. That the play moved to New York. It opens next week, and she's back there with it. But I'm most appreciative of your thinking of my needs for the maybe the tenth of a second you actually did.

(a beat, then)

And by the way? I never spent one minute when I was with her crying on her shoulder.

NORA. I have zero interest in whatever part you might have cried on.

LEE. I spent whatever time I did because it was a palpable relief being with someone who could admit, maybe at just the odd moment now and then, that she could ever possibly be wrong about something.

NORA. And just what is it that I won't admit that I'm so wrong about?

LEE. How 'bout that the real reason you've been marching around so full of noble purpose all this time is because you're trying to make up to Julian for having left him for me!

NORA. Is that what you think?

LEE. That's what I <u>know!</u>

NORA. How quickly we forget.

LEE. Forget what?

NORA. That you stole me away!

LEE. I <u>stole</u> you?

NORA. Let's rewind one more time, okay? Me: a perfectly contented wife with a husband out of town standing alone at the punch bowl at Bernie and Fran's. You: fresh from New York, scoping the party out, then sauntering over to join me.

LEE. I have never sauntered in my life.

NORA. Bullshit.

LEE. I was getting a canapé and you were blocking the way.

NORA. You were checking out my ass.

LEE. That's true.

NORA. And when I turned around, you checked out the rest.

LEE. I checked out <u>everyone</u> in those days.

NORA. You still do, as long as everyone's anyone but me.

LEE. Oh, come off it!

(*after a beat*)

Admit you feel guilty.

NORA. I feel no such thing.

LEE. Not the tiniest, teeniest bit?

NORA. Stop trying to make me feel as though I'm allowed one phone call to my lawyer, okay? I did nothing at all. I was a happily married woman caught up in the grip of a great romancer.

LEE. So it was all me?

NORA. I came along for the ride, but yes, it was mostly you.

LEE. Me and my irresistible charm?

NORA. It's hard to believe, I know, given the way you're behaving right now, but yes! I was powerless in your thrall!

LEE. Oh, I've got a thrall now?

NORA. You did back then. Now, all you've got is a bad attitude and a mouthful of rabbit turds.

(*"sweetly" greeting* **JULIAN** *offstage*)

Julian!

(**JULIAN** *enters. Somewhat weaker now, he moves with the aid of metal walker, cut-off tennis balls attached to its two front legs.*)

NORA. You all right?

JULIAN. Sorry I kept you.

LEE. We put the time to good use.

JULIAN. I was on the phone with Sonia.

LEE. Saint Sonia? Our Lady of the Tentative Offer?

JULIAN. Not anymore she isn't.

    (LEE, NORA look at JULIAN expectantly)

You want the good news or the good news?

LEE. Any kind'll do, Julian. Any kind of good news at all.

JULIAN. The Russians just called her. They've upped their offer!

LEE. Their offer on the condo?

JULIAN. You got it!

NORA. Upped it to what?

LEE. *(overlapping)* To how much?

JULIAN. You ready?

    (a beat, then)

They've gone up to a million three.

LEE. One million three hundred thousand?

JULIAN. That's what she said!

LEE. *(thrilled)* Goddamn, Julian! Congratulations!

NORA. That's fantastic!

LEE. It's sensational! It's amazing!

JULIAN. *(not impressed)* It's a step.

LEE. A step? Julian, it's Mount Everest!

NORA. *(laughs)* At least!

LEE. What did you pay for that place originally? Thirty thousand dollars?

JULIAN. *(emphatically)* <u>Thirty-seven five.</u>

    (a beat, then)

But that was when money had meaning.

LEE. *(almost giddy)* I've got news for you: money's making a comeback!

JULIAN. *(proudly, to NORA)* I told you they'd go higher, didn't I say?

NORA. Absolutely you did.

JULIAN. I knew they were lowballing me.

NORA. You called it, sweetheart.

JULIAN. They were lowballing me then - and they're low-balling me now.

LEE. *(stunned)* ...Eck-fucking-scuse me?

NORA. *(sensing trouble)* Lee.

JULIAN. *(to NORA)* You'll see. In a couple of weeks they'll come up from there. It never hurts to squeeze 'em a little.

LEE. Julian —

NORA. *(to LEE)* He may be right, you know.

JULIAN. I haven't lost it altogether.

NORA. Whoever said you did?

LEE. *(explodes)* Are you people kidding me?

JULIAN. It's worth a try.

LEE. Jesus Jumping Christ!

NORA. *(to LEE)* If he can get a little more for the place, why shouldn't he?

LEE. Nora, we are talking about a sixteen hundred square foot, onebedroom shitbox!

(to JULIAN)

You honestly think you're going to do better than a million three? In today's market?

JULIAN. Taking a beat's the only way to find out.

LEE. A beat?

JULIAN. I just wanna wait it out a little while longer, that's all.

LEE. *(frustration mounting)* A little while longer? I've got your "beat" right here, Julian.

NORA. Lee —

JULIAN. Plus which, I need a little more time to check out the tax ramifications.

LEE. The tax ramifications? The tax ramifications are I am going to ram a fication up your ass if you don't sell your place and get the hell out of mine!

NORA. Lee!

JULIAN. It could be that kind of income is more than I should be taking in in one calendar year, is all!

NORA. Stop! The both of you!

LEE. <u>You</u> stop! I cannot believe you are entertaining this idiocy!

JULIAN. Hey, settle down, okay? Let's have a little tone here.

LEE. I'm sorry, Julian. I ran out of tippytoes weeks - months ago! You go ahead and do whatever the hell you want to do, all right?

(to **NORA***)*

And, not that you need my permission, but you feel free, too. Go for it, the both of you!

JULIAN. I'm just going to have my accountant check it out!

LEE. You do that, Julian. It might very well be that it is better for you not to have that much money come in next year. Or the year after that.

(starting off)

Or maybe you shouldn't even take that offer in this lifetime!

NORA. Where're you going?

LEE. To get the other car!

NORA. It's silly not to go together.

LEE. I'm not going where you're going, Nora.

NORA. You're not coming to lunch?

LEE. Not to lunch, not to dinner, and I'm afraid I've seen my last changing of the Filipino Guard every breakfast, too!

NORA. *(going to him)* Sweetheart, it's Father's Day.

LEE. Perfect. Bring the millionaire.

NORA. Do you have any idea how so completely unlike you this is?

LEE. Maybe it's the guy you <u>think</u> I am that I'm being so completely unlike.

NORA. *(evenly)* Just get in the car. You and I'll talk about this later.

LEE. Haven't you noticed, Nor? Later keeps getting later and later around here. From now on, it can get as later as it wants, okay? Only without me! I'm done!

NORA. Don't do this, Lee.

(touching his arm)

Please.

LEE. Careful. Julian might think there's something's going on between us.

JULIAN. *(to* **LEE***)* I can stay home, if it makes you feel better.

LEE. *(heading for* **JULIAN***)* "Home?" Do I look like someone who would turn a man out of his own house?

NORA. *(blocking* **LEE***'s way)* Don't get physical!

LEE. *(to* **NORA***)* Oh, give me a break!

(facing **JULIAN***)*

I'm sorry I stole Nora away from you, Julian. Okay? There! I finally said it!

JULIAN. Thank you. Thank you, Lee.

LEE. I'm sorry I stole your wife. I'm sorry I stole your <u>life!</u>

(to **NORA***)*

Turns out <u>I'm</u> the one who feels guilty, right?

JULIAN. Guilty about what?

LEE. Name something. I've spent a lifetime feeding that addiction. Here.

(handing **JULIAN** *a key ring)*

I had no absolutely no right to ever come between you!

JULIAN. I don't want your keys.

LEE. *(re: keys)* This one's to the SUV, the one you're not making a dime on. This is for the house. This is for the shed in the back where we keep the boys' pool toys.

JULIAN. *(re: keys)* What's this one for?

NORA. Julian!

JULIAN. *(innocently)* I'm just asking! It's a funny little key!

LEE. That goes to my safety deposit box - where all the love letters Nora sent me while she was still married to you are sitting under a half-inch of very unromantic dust. You can read them together some night when you take a break from mooning over the snapshots of how Cosmopolitan-magazine-happy you were before the big, bad wolf came along, okay? Enjoy!

(to **NORA***)*

And fuck off!

JULIAN. That's a lady you're talking to, Buster.

LEE. *(to* **NORA***, re:* **JULIAN***)* Oh, you're going to love this guy! All over again!

NORA. Where're you going? Don't tell me. New York?

LEE. Still? Now? That part of my life is as over as this one is. You ready for the final blow? I am going to get into the car and I am going to take the freeway - then, driving <u>all the way in reverse</u>, I'm going to hole up in my office at the studio until can I find a place of my own - hopefully one that doesn't reek of Desitin!

NORA. You won't be happy there!

LEE. What's the difference where I'm not? The important thing is I can let you give Julian back the forever you've always thought you stole from him! You can coddle and cuddle him and measure and clock the oh-so-gentle shifts in coloration accumulated in his ever-increasing, already countless pit stops. You can do whatever it takes to make you finally feel better about having dumped him for the master Thrallmeister!

JULIAN. Yelling is bad for me.

LEE. *(loudly)* Shut up, Julian! Volume is all I have left!

(a beat, then)

She's all yours, okay? She's all yours - Take Two!

(He exits.)

(A moment passes.)

(Then:)

JULIAN. *(to* **NORA***)* I'll sell the condo. Get Sonia on the phone. I'll sell.

NORA. No. Don't worry about it. It's too late.

JULIAN. I'm sorry, Nora. Truly.

NORA. *(a beat, then, with a sad smile)* Happy Father's Day, Julian.

(The lights fade.)

(Another passage from the elegy is heard in the process of being composed.)

End of Act One

ACT TWO

Scene One

(The darkness is relieved by the glow of a suddenly-opened cell phone.)

(We hear it being dialed.)

(A beat, then a second cell phone's ringtone is heard and its display offers its dim share of light.)

NORA. *(stage right, on her cell phone)* Billy?

BILLY. *(stage left, on his cell phone, uncomfortably)* I'm downstairs. In Lee's building.

NORA. *(detecting his mood)* You up for this?

BILLY. I'm a lousy liar.

NORA. Just push 3-G, he'll buzz you in.

BILLY. Right.

NORA. *(a beat, then)* Get on with it. I've got a few things to do myself.

(another beat, then)

Billy?

BILLY. Yeah?

NORA. Lying's sometimes the best thing you can do for someone.

(Both cell phone lights disappear.)

Scene Two

(Lights up on a small apartment.)

*(**LEE**, entering in shirt and trousers, hears a rap at the door.)*

LEE. *(calls out)* It's open.

*(On **BILLY**'s entrance:)*

Billy, the Kid!

BILLY. *(uncomfortably)* You ready?

LEE. I'm starved and a half.

(donning a sweater)

I've been at the piano since five this morning. Breakfast was a pack of smoked almonds left over from Kitty Hawk.

BILLY. Ick.

LEE. A bachelor makes do, right?

BILLY. *(ruefully)* Or he doesn't.

(a beat, then)

How's the work coming?

LEE. For your ears only? Without your mother interrupting me, it's hard to get anything done.

(finishes buttoning his own)

Want a sweater? It's nippy out, no?

BILLY. *(a rueful smile)* You sound like Mom.

LEE. *(shrugs)* Personalities are adhesive.

(going to the wall)

The family that sticks together literally sticks together. Let me set the alarm.

BILLY. Lee?

LEE. *(arming the device)* Yeah?

BILLY. You been happy here?

LEE. Don't knock alone. There's lots to be said for living with neighbors you're not married to - or ever were. *Andiamo,* buddy.

BILLY. *(blurting it out)* We're not going where you think we're going, you know.

LEE. I don't follow.

BILLY. *(after getting up the courage)* We're going to your house!

LEE. What do you mean, my house? Your mother's house?

BILLY. The house you used-to, ought-to and're going to move back-into-where-you-belong, that house, that's right!

LEE. *(after a beat)* You lied to me?

BILLY. Not exactly.

LEE. You didn't call and say, "Let's have lunch?"

BILLY. And we're going to. Lotis is making that Filipino stuff you love, those *lumpia* egg roll things.

LEE. Was this the plan when you called me?

BILLY. There was no plan.

LEE. You're lying, Bill.

BILLY. I'm not!

LEE. You don't think I don't know the signs? The minute you walked in here, you've been plucking at your hair like you promised someone you've gotta be bald by midnight! You are lying your head off - literally!

BILLY. Only because Mom told me to!

LEE. When're you gonna learn that sometimes you have to save that woman from herself? Think about it, okay? Have I ever, even once, have I ever lied to you since the day we met?

BILLY. Not to me, no, but you must've told your share of them, or we would never would've been together in the first place!

LEE. You know what, your Honor? Just get out of here, okay? Take a walk. I mean it, Bill!

BILLY. Don't call me "Bill." You only call me that when you're mad at me.

LEE. How about I'm <u>furious</u> with you?

BILLY. How about <u>I</u> am with you?

LEE. With me?

BILLY. With <u>all</u> of you! Enough is finally enough! You and Mom and Dad are just going to have to figure out how to live together under the same goddamn roof again!

LEE. Listen to me, <u>Bill</u>, I have no interest whatsoever in the three of us figuring out how we can become a better couple, or thrupple, or whatever the hell it is that we finally morphed into being! To quote that old English teacher who flunked you once said to me: "I'm sorry, sir, but I have gave it my best!"

BILLY. You guys just don't get it, do you? This is <u>my</u> time to be a mess! You're all supposed to be sitting around in nursing homes, shitting your diapers and singing "Jingle Bells" in the middle of July! But you're all so busy stirring all your old crap up, there's not a day goes by that one of you doesn't call me to bitch about the other two! It's like frigging high school!

LEE. I'm sorry we're all such a drag on you.

BILLY. You should be, damn it!

LEE. How 'bout if we die, would that help? I'd be happy to put at least two of us out of their misery.

BILLY. What I want is for all of you to live like the adults I've always needed you to be! I'm going through absolutely the worst time of my life, and instead of being free to deal with my own problems, I'm busy housebreaking a litter of three completely fucked-up puppies!

LEE. *(after a beat)* What do you mean, the "absolutely the worst" time in your life?

BILLY. I'm getting a divorce.

LEE. *(pained, softly)* Jesus, Billy.

BILLY. Don't tell Mom, okay?

LEE. Mom being Mom, I think it's a pretty safe bet she's going to find out, don't you?

BILLY. I'm going to tell her. I will. Just not yet.

LEE. *(after a beat)* I thought you and Barbara were seeing a counselor.

BILLY. Mom told you?!

LEE. Of course, she told me. She told me the minute she got home the day you told her not to.

BILLY. And you're going to tell her I'm getting divorced, aren't you?

(a beat, then)

Goddamn it, I <u>know</u> you will, even if you give me your word you won't. <u>Especially</u> if you give me your word you won't.

LEE. *(after a beat)* The counseling didn't help?

BILLY. We never went for any. I told Mom we would, but we didn't. You're not supposed to know that.

LEE. It's getting hard to remember all the things I don't.

(a beat, then)

And why didn't you see one, may I ask?

BILLY. I didn't want to! I figured if Barbara wants out, the hell with it.

LEE. Can I make one suggestion?

BILLY. You can suggest all you want. I filed yesterday. It's over! In six months we'll be free. <u>She'll</u> be free.

LEE. Maybe she doesn't want to be.

BILLY. How many ways you wanna have it, Lee?

LEE. Me?

BILLY. You're the one who said she was the type, remember?

LEE. I never said she was the type.

BILLY. You said you knew "the look."

LEE. I <u>do</u> know the look and she <u>is</u> the type, but do <u>you</u> really want this marriage to end? Ending is really ending, you know.

BILLY. Over's likewise over.

LEE. You don't find yourself wishing things were how they were? You don't feel there's something missing you'd love to have back in your life again?

BILLY. What're you making a case for? Mom got divorced when she met you. These things happen.

LEE. From where I stand now, I know they don't always have to.

BILLY. You talk like you and Mom were a mistake.

LEE. *(after a beat)* Maybe I meant for things to turn out a whole lot better than they did. Maybe I've kept on looking for something I already had.

(A long moment passes. A framed snapshot catches **LEE***'s eye.)*

LEE. The night we met –

BILLY. What?

*(***LEE*** *hands him the picture.)*

BILLY. This was the party?

LEE. At Fran and Bernie Michael's.

BILLY. He was a lawyer, you told me.

LEE. Show business mostly. Bernie was smart, fast, top of the line. Atticus Finch on speed. Fran had the first breast reduction in our zip code.

BILLY. And they're both dead now?

LEE. They went a month apart. First, her; then, him. I did their eulogies.

BILLY. Was it one of those "she was the love of his life - after she died he just quietly slipped away" deals?

LEE. Not quite. Fran killed herself.

(a beat, then)

On an inland cruise to Alaska.

BILLY. Why, does anyone know?

LEE. Bernie Michaels would've stuck it in a change purse, a keyhole, anything. The cruise was meant to be the second honeymoon he'd always promise Fran every time she found lipstick on his boxers. Two days out, he started up with a girl from San Diego.

BILLY. A girl?

LEE. In her 60's. And not all that much to look at, from all I heard.

BILLY. Then, why – ?

LEE. The lure of the hunt, maybe. The thrill of the unknown. The idea of coming to someone with a flawless, clean slate. It didn't take long for Fran to find out. It never did. She didn't say "boo." The last night out, she just left him at the blackjack table, went back to their cabin and swallowed half a drug store.

BILLY. Sad.

LEE. Go figure - someone who looked so great in tennis shorts, too.

BILLY. How'd he take it?

LEE. Bernie? Bernie was destroyed. Cheating's no fun when there's no one to cheat on. Anyhow, back then, Fran used to throw these great parties, so she could keep an eye on his wandering one.

BILLY. *(looking at the picture)* Is that Mom in the corner?

LEE. *(nodding)* That's her.

BILLY. And the skinny guy next to her?

LEE. I could use that blazer as a lamp base now.

BILLY. *(studying the photo)* Where's Dad?

LEE. Your father was in Detroit.

BILLY. *(pointing)* Who's that?

LEE. My date.

BILLY. Pretty.

LEE. Pretty strange. Judith Klein.

(musing, a la Cary Grant)

Judy, Judy, Judy.

BILLY. Strange how?

LEE. Sex made her feel guilty. Every time we made out in the place I rented whenever I came out here from New York, the minute her guilt kicked in, she'd hop out of the sack and start in cleaning.

BILLY. Cleaning?

LEE. Dusting, vacuuming. She'd change the linens, wax the floor - whatever it took to make her stop feeling dirty.

BILLY. That's not the worst hang-up ever, I guess.

LEE. Are you kidding, she used to save me a fortune!

BILLY. So you showed up with Judy – ?

LEE. In my freshly-washed car. And then, I saw her.

BILLY. Mom?

LEE. I saw those big, brown, beautiful eyes across the crowded room.

BILLY. Like the song.

LEE Like the song. Exactly like the song.

(recalling)

God, that first look felt so inevitable. So indelible. It still plays in my head like a freeze frame. One look and it felt like I'd found a part of myself I never knew was missing. Twenty minutes later, we were on the floor, locked inside Fran's walk-in closet.

BILLY. Making out?

LEE. No, no, no. Talking. Finishing each other's sentences. Sharing memories. Aware we were starting a new one from scratch. You know that feeling when two people are both inside that invisible, vibrating space?

BILLY. *(after a respectful beat)* Sounds like a movie.

LEE. It felt like one. Your mother even scored it.

BILLY. She what?

LEE. Well, she knew I was a composer, so that's two brownie points right off the bat. Writing movie scores was certainly more exotic than the car leasing business.

(aside)

No offense.

BILLY. *(none taken)* Tell me about it.

LEE. *(continuing his story)* The next day, she called and sang me a song over the phone. A ballad, she said she'd written the minute she got home from the party.

BILLY. I didn't know she could do that.

LEE. She didn't. A couple of nights later I heard it on the radio.

BILLY. The same song?

LEE. Note for note. Word for word.

BILLY. Mom's song ended up on the air?

LEE. It wasn't her song!

BILLY. She lied to you?

LEE. Completely. Knowing from talking to her how lying really wasn't her thing, I knew how serious she was about our being together. It actually sealed the deal in a strange way.

BILLY. She wanted you to want her.

LEE. She had no idea how automatic that feeling had been.

BILLY. So then?

LEE. So then?

(after a beat)

So then we had an affair.

(another beat)

Damn it, I was never going to tell you that.

BILLY. For how long, the affair?

LEE. Almost two years.

BILLY. And Dad never knew?

LEE. He's always said he didn't. I believe him. It made things easier, I guess. Harder, too.

BILLY. How'd he find out?

LEE. Your mom told him. Little by agonizing little.

BILLY. It really shut him down, I think.

LEE. Ended him, really. That's why, if you have even the slightest desire to reach over at night and wrap yourself around Barbara - only her - you've got to give the both of you another chance. Your mom was totally, completely in love with me in the beginning, but it's never been that simple ever since. Not for her. Not for me. Certainly not for your dad, who I'm sure wishes he'd tried a whole lot harder to hold on to the life they'd had. God knows their breakup's given you your own share of collateral damage to deal with, but don't add to the shrapnel, Billy, but give it another try at home. You deserve a better future.

BILLY. *(after some thought)* Only if you'll let me take you to your house for lunch. That's the deal. I'm sorry. That's the deal.

LEE. *(a beat, then) Lumpia*, huh?

BILLY. Fresh-made. Each one's a killer from Manila.

LEE. *(after another beat)* Let me set the alarm.

(after punching in the code)

We're outta here.

BILLY. *(stopping at the door)* Lee?

LEE. We've only got sixty seconds.

BILLY. You said before that Mom's eyes were brown when you met her?

LEE. They were.

BILLY. But her eyes are as green as yours are.

LEE. Now, they're green. Back then, they were brown.

BILLY. They changed color?

LEE. Over the years, they did, yes.

BILLY. How's that possible?

LEE. Possible doesn't enter into it. It's what happened. Like I said, pal: Adhesive.

(As a troubled iteration of the elegy plays:)

(The light fades.)

Scene Three

(Late afternoon.)

(The Baers' morning room.)

(LEE *loads an archive box stuffed with copies of dog-eared* Reader's Digests *and old crossword puzzle magazines.)*

(A heavily dressed **JULIAN**, *wearing a Band-Aid on the bridge of his nose, is writing a check.)*

LEE. You must have every *Reader's Digest* ever published.

JULIAN. "Throw them out," Nora'd say. How do you throw old friends out you know on every page?

LEE. *(after a beat, re* **JULIAN** *'s effort)* You don't really have to do this, Julian.

(JULIAN *waves the check he's been writing to dry his signature before offering it to* **LEE.** *)*

JULIAN. This should cover everything. If not, you know where I'll be.

LEE. *(looking at the check)* This is not going to make her happy.

JULIAN. Who is she to be happy all the time?

LEE. *(pocketing the check)* You're as good as your word.

JULIAN. You thought this day would never come, I bet.

LEE. *(with a smile)* It did cross my mind now and then, but you really don't have to go, y'know.

JULIAN. Would you deny me the pleasure of an assisted existence? Of the pleasures of watching waves and homeless people humping under the palms?

LEE. *(a beat, then)* How's your nose?

JULIAN. It'll live. If anybody asks, I'll say I had a little work done on it.

LEE. I can't tell you how sorry I am about what happened at lunch last week. Whatever it was that got into me that made it all turn so ugly.

JULIAN. What's the big mystery? After putting up with me so long, I finally got into you.

(reflects)

There's a time when a year is just so much petty cash. The older you get, it's like the good years forgot your address. Never mind the bad ones. They never know when to leave at all.

(after another a beat)

Marriage is a tough enough proposition for two people. You throw another set of feelings into the mix and pretty soon you get homesick for the life you used to think was impossible.

LEE. Still, I never should have had so much wine.

JULIAN. Don't worry about it.

(looking at his watch)

Has the woman ever been on time? Ever? For anything?

LEE. It helps feeling that nothing really starts until you get there.

JULIAN. In her case, who can blame her?

(fingering his books fondly)

Even stuff I've read I don't know how many times over, I can never wait to find out what happens next. Now, it's <u>my</u> next chapter I haven't got a clue about.

(A car horn sounds offstage)

LEE. That's her.

JULIAN. *(checks his watch)* Right off the button.

(The light fades.)

(The elegy, nearing its completed form, is heard.)

Scene Four

(Santa Monica. Just before sunset.)

*(**NORA** wears a lightweight track suit.)*

*(**JULIAN** is dressed as he was in the previous scene.)*

NORA. This is wrong, Julian. I can't tell you how wrong it is.

JULIAN. Trust me, Nora. I'm a professor in wrong, but I know this is right for me. The minute they load in my bed, I'll be a free man again.

NORA. But in your heart of hearts you know it's a mistake.

JULIAN. So I'll learn. I've got my whole life ahead of me. I'm only 73.

NORA. What you are is stubborn, stubborn, stubborn.

JULIAN. And how about lucky?

(off her look)

You heard the receptionist. Mine is the last apartment left with a window on the beach. They're going like hotcakes. There must be old geezers all over town seeking asylum from vase-throwing second husbands. Who knew?

NORA. That was so unlike him.

JULIAN. *In vino veritas.* The truth is what made him blow like a volcano.

NORA. Just because something's Latin doesn't mean it's true.

JULIAN. He <u>needed</u> to get mad.

(after a beat)

A year of living with the Ghost of Marriage Past, one year, Nora. I never should have allowed it to happen.

(another beat, then)

But I liked it. I liked being with you. You always made me feel part of the family.

NORA. Turnabout's fair play.

(looking off)

Let me tell them to take the bed back.

(a plea)

Julie?

JULIAN. I gave Lee a check for it.

NORA. For the Tempur-pedic? Why did you do that?

JULIAN. Consider it a lease-to-own.

NORA. It was meant as a gift, you know that.

JULIAN. You want only my good for me? Let me pay for my own sleep. It'll be a whole lot deeper that way.

(looking around)

Remember how we used to drive out here to catch the sunset?

NORA. You used to say, "Let's go drive to where the country ends."

JULIAN. I had my moments.

NORA. More than you think.

(They walk along.)

JULIAN. Funny, huh? Me <u>and</u> the country both ending up in the same spot?

NORA. I just want so much for it all to turn out well for you.

JULIAN. Guess what, okay? As of this minute, how things turn out for me is officially no longer your problem.

NORA. How will you get along? Who's going to cook for you?

JULIAN. Lotis.

NORA. You've talked to her? You've been planning this?

JULIAN. No, but I'm sure she'll come and scramble some eggbeaters for a couple of thousand dollars a day. I'll get by, Nora. Life goes on, did you hear about it? Life's got a mind of its own.

(A long moment passes.)

JULIAN. I'm off your plate now, you should be happy.

NORA. Having you "off my plate" doesn't make me happy. At all.

JULIAN. Why the hell would you want me around? And around? And around?

NORA. Why do you think? Because I care what happens to you?

JULIAN. <u>Now</u>, you care. Now, that I'm a little human dish you can drop pity in whenever you feel rotten. That's not caring. That's charity - mostly for yourself. You just want me all tucked in and snuggled in your house, so whenever you're in the mood you can be all giving and caring, or we can play "remember when we this" or "remember when we that," or we can talk about Billy or about the boys. You don't want to let me go.

NORA. Julian, I let you go long ago.

JULIAN. You left in such dribs and drabs a person would have had to speed up the film ten times to see what was happening. By the time you finally told me you weren't coming home from New York, the life we had had already melted!

NORA. Because you let it! You just accepted my leaving!

JULIAN. I didn't know you were leaving me for him.

NORA. I had no idea I would.

JULIAN. Why burn a bridge until you get to it, huh?

NORA. Not at all.

JULIAN. Wait a minute, wait a minute! Let's back up here a second!

NORA. What?

JULIAN. I didn't accept your leaving? Are you saying it's my fault we're not together?

NORA. Well?

JULIAN. *(pointing)* And what a beautiful moon the sun is up there, right?

NORA. That's not what I meant.

JULIAN. You said you wanted to go to New York and act
on the stage. I said yes, good husband that I was. Any
good husband that was also a schmuck. You said Billy
was better off being with you - a boy needs his mother,
to which I agreed. Why be <u>half</u> a schmuck, right?

NORA. Did you ever once ask, "Why?" Did you ever say,
"The hell you're going! I'm not losing you, goddamn
it?!"

JULIAN. You are amazing. You make a man eat crow, and
then you want him to ask for seconds?

NORA. But not a peep out of you? Just the acceptance that
if that's what it was then you were all right with that's
what it was?

JULIAN. You know me! You know I'm not a person who
wears his pain on the outside!

(a beat, then)

You suffer in silence long enough, it doesn't feel like
suffering anymore. It feels like - elegance. Like you're
at the best table at the best restaurant in town.
Spilling your guts about your disappointments or your
heartbreaks, that becomes the suffering. However nuts
it sounds, hurting almost keeps you, I don't know, it like
keeps you warm. Like you've got a private little garden
inside where you bury all your grief. I'm not talking
self-pity here. I'm not talking about pity at all. I'm
saying my way is to swallow whatever happens, because
most of the time what the hell can you do about what
other people are going to do to you anyway?

(a beat, then)

When you left me like you did, when you pulled our
life together apart, thread by thread, I thought, if this
is what she's capable of when she's happy, what the
hell's she going to do to us if she ever gets sad?

(after a beat)

One thing <u>I'll</u> never understand, okay? Why him?

NORA. Why Lee?

JULIAN. Why this - this -

(sneers)

This guy? It's not exactly like you left me for Tyrone Power, you know. He's nice enough, I'll give you that. But you left me for <u>him?</u>

(after a beat)

I did everything for you. Provided. Remembered every occasion. Listened every day when you came back from the set with your rambling stories. Why him?

*(**NORA** takes her time before answering.)*

NORA. I can't say it.

JULIAN. You want me to fight for you? This is as good as it's going to get. Tell me why you left me for him.

NORA. *(after a very long beat)* He made me feel a way that I'd never felt before.

JULIAN. Because he was younger than I was? Than <u>you</u> were by what, three or four years?

NORA. Two.

JULIAN. Because he was more from your world than I was? More entertaining? More exciting? Cleverer? Because he's no more of a man than I am.

NORA. No, he's not. You're right about that. He's not.

JULIAN. So what the hell was it?

NORA. *(after a beat)* There's a way a man comes to you in life, Julian, a way he places himself in your path that wakes you up - makes you feel you're living the life you really came here to live. Like you were somewhere else altogether, and you came here for <u>this</u>. You came here for the two of you. Like the world won't be right if you weren't together. Like everything, even your sanity, depends on it.

JULIAN. And I never made you feel that way? Not ever?

NORA. *(after a long beat)* You made me feel a lot of things. Wonderful things. Safe. Secure. Settled. But never that. No. I have to be honest with you. Never that.

JULIAN. And you felt it with him?

NORA. I did. Back then. I really did. I'm not even sure why now. Maybe it's not so much that he needed me. Maybe I needed him. Or we needed us. We needed there to be an us.

(after a beat)

I'm sorry.

JULIAN. No, no, no. Feelings like that are real. I know. I felt them when I was with you.

(a beat, then)

People talk, Nora. I know it hasn't been easy for you.

NORA. *(quietly)* Thank you, people.

JULIAN. The bed of roses getting a little bit crowded?

NORA. I deal with it. I think of it as the tax on my happiness.

(a beat, then)

Let me take you home, Julian.

JULIAN. Whatever happens, I can't ever go back there.

NORA. *(suddenly overcome, quietly)* Oh, God.

JULIAN. What?

NORA. The thought of something happening to you all on your own here –

JULIAN. I was with my father when he died.

NORA. I wasn't talking about you dying.

JULIAN. Yes, you were. It's all right. I lived through my father's death, I'll live through my own. You know what I mean. All being there when it happens is is give you a better idea of what helpless is. He died at Cedars.

NORA. I know.

JULIAN. The place is getting to be the village square.

NORA. Don't make jokes.

JULIAN. *(after a beat)* It was like watching someone very slowly drown, and you're sitting right there and you can't do anything about it, because the water that's rising isn't water at all. It's Time. And you can't stop it. There's no drain in the floor you can open up to let the Time out. It just keeps rising and rising.

(after a beat)

And I would think about it, my own days when I was there. "What happens when it's my turn to go? Who's gonna be there to turn to, to say, "Wow. I lived. I lived and it was really something.""

Some things went right, some things didn't. It's not like I'd know how to make it any better if there was a next time.

(after another beat)

Just knowing you'd want to be there when it happens is more of a gift than I would ever have expected.

(Lights fade.)

(A quartet plays **LEE**'s *completed elegy.)*

Scene Five

(A harsh, windy day.)

(Suited and necktied, **LEE** *joins the waiting* **NORA**.*)*

(Like **LEE**, *she is in dark clothing.)*

(The mood is melancholy and distant.)

(These two are not on solid ground with one another yet.)

LEE. *(gently)* How you doing, kid?

NORA. Would have been nice if a few more people had shown up.

LEE. You want a big crowd? Die young.

NORA. *(after a beat)* All the men wore ties.

LEE. I sent out a mass e-mail last night.

NORA. *(after a beat)* You see Joe Slotkin?

LEE. I couldn't look at him.

NORA. Chemo.

LEE. Yep.

NORA. What a dancer that man was. Nobody could dip like Joe Slotkin.

LEE. I think Joe's all dipped out. His doctor gave him less than a month.

NORA. To be honest, I was a little surprised he got up to leave at the end.

LEE. "It hardly pays to go home from here."

NORA. *(with a smile at the familiar punchline)* Right.

(after a beat)

I may have overdone it on the food at the house.

LEE. It'll all go. Eating's still the second best way to prove you're alive.

NORA. *(after a long beat)* The piece was beautiful, Lee. It's the best thing you've ever done.

LEE. Thanks. It seemed to work.

NORA. Even with just the quartet, it really came through.

LEE. It sure beat giving another eulogy.

NORA. You'll still say a few words at mine, won't you?

LEE. God willing, I won't be there. You know what I mean.

NORA. *(after a beat, smiles)* "God willing."

LEE. What?

NORA. Ever notice how often "God" springs to your lips whenever we're out here?

LEE. Never hurts to kiss a little ass.

NORA. *(looking off)* Should I get Billy?

LEE. Let him be. He and Julian can use the time together.

(A moment passes.)

NORA. I could just kill myself.

LEE. Give yourself a break.

NORA. Of all the days to get my nails done.

LEE. How were you supposed to know?

NORA. I should have. This past month he could've gone at any minute, all his doctors said.

LEE. Like they're not going to cover all their bets? Overrated as it is, Julian had the last laugh. He got to die in his sleep. In a Tempur-pedic, no less.

NORA. Beats doing it in the village square.

LEE. Pardon?

NORA. Something Julian said. Unimportant.

(after a beat)

And whose bed were <u>you</u> in when Billy had you paged?

(after a beat)

He said you were with somebody. I assume it was her.

LEE. We were not in bed.

(after a beat)

Marla and I have not -

NORA. *(cuts him off)* It's none of my business.

LEE. She and I have not <u>anything</u> - not one single thing, since the day I moved out. I told you she was never the reason I left when I did.

NORA. Do me a favor? I am barely able to admit her existence as a pronoun. Mentioning her by name puts
a face on her, and that makes me want to grab her
by one of her extensions and hurl her into the first
freshly-dug, wormiest grave I can find.

LEE. *(quietly)* Gotcha.

NORA. *(after a beat)* She must have been devastated by the
reviews in New York.

LEE. She was, a little.

NORA. How'd she take the news about Julian?

LEE. This may come as a shock, but we never did spend a
lot of time talking about Julian.

(after a beat, looking off)

What'd <u>he</u> say? Did you ever tell him?

NORA. About you –

LEE. About me and -

(diplomatically)

The aforesaid pronoun person.

NORA. Julian knew.

LEE. You told him?

NORA. It's a small town, remember?

LEE. What'd he say about it?

NORA. Not a whole lot. I think the last thing in the world
he wanted was having some reason to feel sorry for me.

LEE. *(looking off)* I wonder if he knew how much I liked him.

NORA. <u>That</u> was certainly the best-kept secret of the war.
Especially after you threw the vase at his head.

LEE. I was aiming for the wall.

NORA. And his nose just came hurtling out of nowhere?

LEE. Can we please not mention that particular afternoon
ever again? I know you never saw it that way, but for
the most part, I tried to be on my best behavior whenever Julian and I were together.

NORA. Well, your worst behavior was pretty miserable.

LEE. As previously noted.

NORA. Not to mention the way you rarely talked to him.

LEE. Not to mention.

NORA. So how do you explain the best behavior - if and when there was ever such an occurrence?

LEE. I guess I didn't want him to think that you'd left him - that he'd come in in second place to some kind of Bernie Michaels.

NORA. What hurts more - the truth or a lie?

LEE. Six'a one, I guess.

(a beat, then)

Billy may be having a hard time saying goodbye.

NORA. He's a good man.

LEE. He is. In spite of me.

NORA. Come on now. He thinks of you in ways he never did about his father.

LEE. I look at him and I see all those little step-genes I've passed on: the insecurity; the quiet rage that's sometimes not all that quiet - the lifelong effects of a life-changing decision that no one ever bothered to ask him to approve.

NORA. Kids survive.

LEE. Until they grow up, they do.

*(**BILLY** appears, his suit jacket draped over his arm.)*

BILLY. Sorry.

(still a bit choked)

I guess I got a little –

NORA. If you want to stay longer –

LEE. We'll hang with you, if you like.

BILLY. I'm fine.

(after a beat)

I just didn't want to leave without telling him, you know?

(another beat)

BILLY. *(cont.)* About the divorce.

(sheepishly)

Pretty chicken way to do it, I know.

LEE. We can only do what we can.

(Another long moment passes.)

BILLY. It struck me, talking to him: looking down... thinking –

NORA. *(taking his hand)* Thinking what, sweetheart?

BILLY. Thinking, didn't you just pick me up off the ground at the pony rides, Pop? Wasn't it just a few minutes ago that you covered my eyes at the movies to protect me from a six-inch tall T. rex?

(a beat, then)

It goes by so fast.

LEE. It's a rocket.

(The three of them stand silent a moment. Then, as **BILLY** *puts his jacket on:)*

BILLY. I'm going to pick up Barbara and bring her to the house.

NORA. I thought you signed the papers last week.

BILLY. I did. I just want her there with me.

LEE. You two talking?

BILLY. Not yet. But I just texted her. She texted back. It's a start.

LEE. Starts are the best.

NORA. What about the tool belt guy?

BILLY. He's doing the house next door now.

(a beat; then, to **LEE***)*

I figure we are worth another chance. And all the boys are trying to do is grow up. Guess the same goes for me, right?

LEE. Maybe for all of us.

BILLY. *(kissing* **NORA***)* Mom.

(turning, embracing **LEE***)*

Your piece was wonderful.

LEE. Thanks, Billy.

BILLY. Wasn't it, Mom?

NORA. *(to* **LEE***)* Wonderful.

BILLY. *(starting to leave)* I'll see you guys at the house.

LEE. Good luck.

NORA. *(calls after him)* Be nice.

*(***BILLY***'s exit leaves* **LEE** *and* **NORA** *alone once more.)*

LEE. Go figure.

(a beat, then)

I'd like to come home, Nor.

NORA. Now, that I'm short one husband?

LEE. Take a chance, okay? Divorces don't seem to be working out around here. Maybe marriage can make a comeback.

NORA. Is this a kind of proposal?

LEE. Sounds like it to me.

NORA. In a graveyard?

LEE. *(another beat, then)* Do you have the slightest inkling how much there still is left for you and me to disagree about? You are my fucking oxygen, babe. Sometimes the head winds are a little strong - but it's you - and way too often you alone - who keeps us airborne. You're the mortar in this marriage. You're my melody. You're my tempo. And take it from someone who's written a few stretches of music in his time, the best love song I ever heard was the one you wrote for me.

NORA. I didn't write it.

LEE. The way I heard it, you did.

NORA. ...See?

LEE. What?

NORA. This is the guy I fell for twenty-five years ago.

LEE. Mister Thrall.

NORA. This is the kind of talk that got me into trouble in the first place.

LEE. It hasn't all been trouble, has it?

NORA. No. Not all of it. But do you realize this is a married woman you're talking to like this? You do realize that I'm someone's wife?

LEE. I did the first time. I just always took it on faith that you were born mine.

(a beat, then)

What do you say? Can I come home?

NORA. *(after a moment)* Not all the way, just yet. Not all at once.

LEE. Whatever you say.

NORA. *(another moment, then)* How about if we start in the closet?

(As they look at one another, the light fades.)

(The final version of **LEE** *'s elegy is heard.)*

End of Play.

Also by
Larry Gelbart...

Abrogate

Floodgate

Mastergate

Sly Fox

Please visit our website **samuelfrench.com** for complete descriptions and licensing information.